CREATIVE GOD
COLORFUL US

CREATIVE GOD
COLORFUL US

TRILLIA NEWBELL

WITH PAINTINGS BY CHASE WILLIAMSON

MOODY PUBLISHERS

CHICAGO

Some content in the section "4 Reasons to Enjoy Our Differences" was adapted from the author's blog: trillianewbell.com.

Unless otherwise indicated, all Scripture quotations are from the ESV® Bible (The Holy Bible, English Standard Version®), copyright © 2001 by Crossway, a publishing ministry of Good News Publishers. Used by permission. All rights reserved.

Scripture quotations marked (NIV) are taken from the Holy Bible, New International Version®, NIV®. Copyright © 1973, 1978, 1984, 2011 by Biblica, Inc.™ Used by permission of Zondervan. All rights reserved worldwide. www.zondervan.com The "NIV" and "New International Version" are trademarks registered in the United States Patent and Trademark Office by Biblica, Inc.™

Scripture quotations marked (GNT) are from the Good News Translation in Today's English Version-Second Edition Copyright © 1992 by American Bible Society. Used by Permission.

Scripture quotations marked (NLT) are taken from the Holy Bible, New Living Translation, copyright ©1996, 2004, 2015 by Tyndale House Foundation. Used by permission of Tyndale House Publishers, a Division of Tyndale House Ministries, Carol Stream, Illinois 60188. All rights reserved.

All emphasis in Scripture has been added.

Published in association with Don Gates, THE GATES GROUP @ www.the-gates-group.com.

Edited by Amanda Cleary Eastep
Cover and Interior Design: Erik M. Peterson
Cover and start of chapter paintings: Chase Williamson
Illustration Credits: 14. MitchMade/Lightstock, 15. Neilras/Shutterstock, 16. Cienpies Design/Shutterstock, 17. Colourhand/Shutterstock, 18. MitchMade/Lightstock, 21. Chase Williamson, 29. Irina Vaneeva/Shutterstock, 33. Lunarts Studio/Shutterstock, 38. MitchMade/Lightstock, 39a. PCH-vector/iStock, 39b. Rudall30/Shutterstock, 40. Rudall30/Shutterstock, 53. Yuoak/iStock, 56. Yuoak/iStock, 63. Qvasimodo/iStock, 64. Qvasimodo/iStock, 66. Julie August/iStock, 72. Iconic Bestiary/Shutterstock, 73. Iconic Bestiary/Shutterstock, 75. MitchMade/Lightstock, 76. MitchMade/Lightstock, 88. MitchMade/Lightstock, 89. MitchMade/Lightstock, 91. MitchMade/Lightstock, 108. Tetiana Lazunova/iStock

Library of Congress Cataloging-in-Publication Data

Names: Newbell, Trillia J., author.
Title: Creative God, colorful us / Trillia Newbell.
Description: Chicago : Moody Publishers, [2021] | Includes bibliographical
   references. | Summary: "God could have made us all exactly the same, but
   He didn't. And our differences are good! This short, colorful book
   (written with grade-schoolers in mind) will share the truth about how we
   were made, our differences, our sin problem, God's rescue, and how we
   should be motivated to love one another on earth"-- Provided by
   publisher.
Identifiers: LCCN 2020040825 (print) | LCCN 2020040826 (ebook) | ISBN
   9780802424181 | ISBN 9780802499844 (ebook)
Subjects: LCSH: Identity (Psychology)--Religious
   aspects--Christianity--Juvenile literature. | Individual
   differences--Religious aspects--Christianity--Juvenile literature. |
   Individuality--Juvenile literature. | Theological
   anthropology--Christianity--Juvenile literature. |
   Salvation--Christianity--Juvenile literature.
Classification: LCC BV4509.5 .N485 2021 (print) | LCC BV4509.5 (ebook) |
   DDC 230--dc23
LC record available at https://lccn.loc.gov/2020040825
LC ebook record available at https://lccn.loc.gov/2020040826

Printed by: Versa Press, Inc. in East Peoria, IL, December 2020

Originally delivered by fleets of horse-drawn wagons, the affordable paperbacks from D. L. Moody's publishing house resourced the church and served everyday people. Now, after more than 125 years of publishing and ministry, Moody Publishers' mission remains the same—even if our delivery systems have changed a bit. For more information on other books (and resources) created from a biblical perspective, go to: www.moodypublishers.com or write to:

Moody Publishers
820 N. LaSalle Boulevard
Chicago, IL 60610

1 3 5 7 9 10 8 6 4 2

Printed in the United States of America

To my kids and the next generation:

God made you and it was good. He sings over you with gladness.

Remember the Lord all the days of your life.

Keep His words you read in the Bible in your heart and do good to all.

I am praying for you to be a generation that shines brightly in our world!

CONTENTS

INTRODUCTION

I WROTE YOU A LETTER!

Hello!

My name is Trillia. I have children who are about your age. They read the book you are holding, and they liked it. So, I thought I'd share it with you too! Thank you for choosing to read *Creative God, Colorful Us*. I am so excited about all the things we will discover.

Growing up, I had many questions about the world and all the people that filled the earth. I wondered who made us. I wondered why people didn't always get along. I used to wish that there would be peace on the earth but couldn't figure out why it didn't happen. Then I started reading the Bible, and so much started to make sense to me.

The Bible is God's Word. It is used for helping people see right from wrong. Most of all, the Bible is where God chose to teach us about Himself (2 Timothy 3:16–17).[1] It is the most important book on the earth. We will be guided by the Bible to learn what God has told us about Himself and people.

In this book, we will answer questions like the ones I had as a kid and the same ones you might have now. I don't want to spoil it by sharing the answers yet. But if you look at the page labeled **CONTENTS,** you can see all that we will explore together—ideas like: the image of God, the fall, the Good News, and more. Don't worry if you don't know what any of those ideas are now. You will as you keep reading.

If you run into a word you don't know, look at the **HELPFUL WORDS TO KNOW** in the back of the book. That's where you will find definitions of the **RED** words throughout the book.

At the end of each chapter, there are a few questions to help you think about what you've read. Those questions are labeled **WHAT DO YOU THINK?** Feel free to write out your answers and share them with a friend or guardian. You can make it fun and answer the questions in a special journal. There are other fun features throughout the book, including thought bubbles, **THE BIG IDEA** summaries of the chapter, and short activities.

When you are finished reading the book, let your parent or guardian know that I wrote them a short letter, too. It's also in the back of the book. Oh, and one more thing: this book is short! There are only seven chapters. My kids were happy to know that. 🙂

I am praying that you will enjoy *Creative God, Colorful Us*!

Trillia

CHAPTER 1

GOD MADE YOU (AND HE MADE YOUR FRIENDS TOO!)

My daughter is fascinated with outer space. She loves to try to find constellations like the Big Dipper and gets excited when there's a full moon. The universe is massive and **DIVERSE**. That means it's huge and filled with many different objects. There are stars and moons and planets and black holes and a bunch of other stuff I can't even imagine!

When you look up at the sky, what do you think about?

WHEN YOU LOOK UP AT THE SKY, WHAT DO YOU THINK ABOUT?

Looking up at the sky reminds me of Psalm 8:3–4:

> When I consider your heavens,
>   the work of your fingers,
> the moon and the stars,
>   which you have set in place,
> what is mankind that you are mindful of them,
>   human beings that you care for them? (NIV)

At the beginning of time, God created the heavens. He set it all in place. He thought of the idea of Mars—the planet that's also called the red planet. God created the moon that shines bright in the night. God created stars that appear to twinkle. God created the sun that warms the earth throughout the year. God did all of this.

Have you ever created something from scratch? It's hard to create from nothing (only God can do that!). Whether it's drawing a picture or writing a story, creating is a lot of work. Because God is powerful and full of knowledge, I don't think it was hard for God to create the world, but it was a lot of work.

AND HE KEPT CREATING.

He created water that would cover the earth—oceans, rivers, and lakes. He created land with mountains and valleys and deserts and plains. And He made sure the land had plants and flowers and trees. And He didn't create just one type of plant or flower or tree; there are thousands of different types!

AND HE KEPT CREATING.

God created animals, lots and lots of animals. He created the giraffe with an incredibly long neck. And He created elephants with their massive trunks. He created lions, which are just really, really big cats. He created fish in the sea, too many to number. He created every insect and bug—those that slither on the ground and those that fly in the air.

God created all of these things, and the Bible tells us that when He was done creating these things, He said at least three times that what He created was good (Genesis 1:10, 18, 25).[1]

God could have stopped creating. God was happy and didn't need anything. But the land needed to be taken care of, kind of like a farmer or a gardener cares for their land (Genesis 2:5).[2] Because God is good and kind, He decided to create people to work the land and care for the animals and begin having children and families to fill the earth.

Maybe you've heard the story of Adam and Eve. God created Adam, the first man, out of the dust on the ground. After Adam was created, God placed him in a garden known as Eden. Eden had everything Adam needed for food and for living a good, long life. Eden was beautiful. Adam got to work caring for the land and all that God had given him. But Adam needed some help and couldn't take care of all the responsibility the Lord gave him on his own.

SO, GOD KEPT CREATING.

God took one of Adam's ribs and crafted a woman. When God was finished, Adam was so happy! Adam and Eve were the first man and woman, and they were also the first husband and wife. They enjoyed each other so much. They loved each other perfectly. They had so much fun in the Garden.

God wanted Adam and Eve to take care of the Garden of Eden so that it could grow and grow to become even more beautiful and big. Eventually, the whole earth was supposed to be like the Garden of Eden. The whole earth would be filled up with God's truth and beauty and goodness. Even though God didn't need anything, He didn't want to do this special job by Himself.

That's why God did something very special when He created humans. Adam and Eve were not like the other creatures He created. God made humans different from the animals. He made them in His own image. That means you and I reflect different characteristics of God Himself!

> So God created mankind
> in his own image,
> in the image of God
> he created them;
> male and female he created them.
> (Genesis 1:27 NIV)

The idea that you are made in the **IMAGE OF GOD** might be hard to understand, but it's true. Since God made everything—the earth, the stars, the whole universe—He gets to be in charge of everything. God is the King of all creation. And when God made us in His image, He gave us the amazing task of being His partners in His special mission. What's His special mission? God wants to fill the whole earth with His glory! That means that God wants the whole world to know and love all of His perfect ways.

Every person walking on this earth and every person that ever lived is made to reflect God. Like a mirror reflects our own image, we reflect the image of God to one another.

THE BIG IDEA

Every person is made by God and in the image of God and therefore is equal in value and worth.

For example:

GOD IS KIND—you can be kind too.

GOD IS LOVING—you can be loving too.

GOD IS FAIR—you can be fair too.

GOD IS FORGIVING—you can be forgiving too.

GOD IS TRUTHFUL—you can be truthful too.

GOD IS WISE—you can be wise too.

GOD IS GOOD—you can do good too.

God is all those things and more, and we can be all those things too. That is how we reflect God. Animals can be fun to play with or loveable or even gentle, but they can't really be truthful or forgiving or fair. Only we can be those things. That's what makes us a special part of God's earth. We are not like other animals. We reflect God.

A friend of mine once wrote, "The Bible does not begin with the creation of a special race of people."*

You know what that means? Every person, from every background, no matter what their skin color is or what they look like, no matter whether they can walk, run, or crawl . . . every person is made by God and every person is made equally. God doesn't have favorites! Isn't that such good news?

God made you. He loved making you. God makes some people tall and some people, like me, short. He makes

---

* J. Daniel Hays, *From Every Tribe and Nation: A Biblical Theology of Race* (Downers Grove, IL: InterVarsity, 2003), 48.

some people with dark skin and some people with lighter skin. He makes some people with straight hair and some people with curly hair. He makes some people with big eyes and some people with small eyes. He

makes some people with birthmarks and some people with freckles. He makes some people with different abilities. God makes all sorts of people. God makes boys and God makes girls. God made everything about you—you are wonderfully made (Psalm 139:14).[3] We are all important to God because He took time to create us. He is a good God!

We are all made in the image of God, so we all have value and are important to God. Understanding that God made you, your friends, your family, and every person you'll ever meet should help you see others as God sees you.

But as you probably already know, all true stories have a beginning, a middle, and an end. The creation of Adam and Eve is a wonderful story. But it isn't the end of their story. What happened next is the reason why it is so hard for us to see each other the way we should. Sometimes we don't like each other. Sometimes we get angry. Sometimes we are mean. This is all because of sin. But God always had a plan to rescue us.

But before we find out how, let's pause and think about what we just read.

WHAT DO YOU THINK?

Here are some questions for you to think about. You can write out your answers in a notebook or journal or talk about your answers with others.

1 How are you different from animals?

2 You and all your friends and every other person ever created by God are made in the image of God. Write what you think that means in your own words.

3 Since every person is made by God, how do you think we should treat each other?

4 Think about the fact that God made you and loved making you. If you wrote a letter to God thanking Him, what would you say?

Here's a prayer I'd write to God for making us:

God, You are so awesome! You are creative and made so many good things. Thank You, God, for making people. Thank You that You had the idea of making people from all over the world with different skin colors and different languages. Thank You for being so kind and so loving. You made all creation, and it is beautiful. Thank You for giving us so much to enjoy. You are good. I love You. Amen.

Do you remember the big idea of this chapter? Look back at The Big Idea. Sing it, rap it, or chant it so that you can remember it. Then share it with a friend!

ACTIVITY

Take a blank piece of paper (or a paper plate) and write "I'm made in the image of God" at the top. Then draw your face on the paper. You can color it or paint it and add yarn, cotton balls, or stickers. Get creative! In the space around your face, write down words that describe the way God made you (example: funny, smart, curly hair, straight hair). Also, write down words that describe what God wants us to be like so that we can reflect Him (example: kind, fair, loving).

REMEMBER: God loved to make you, and He made you on purpose. You are made in His image.

CHAPTER 2

WHEN EVERYTHING WENT WRONG

We know that God created people in His image. God created people who would love Him and love each other—perfectly. But we know that we don't love each other perfectly. We make fun of people. We hurt people. We get angry and fuss and fight. Sometimes we get jealous and want the things our friends have. We do bad things sometimes. So, what went wrong? What happened to the wonderful Garden and the happy people we met in the last chapter? Why aren't we perfectly good all the time?

Adam and Eve's story continued in the Garden, but not in the way you might expect. The two were placed in a beautiful garden with the freedom to enjoy laughing and eating and working and resting. They had everything they needed to live a long and happy life together. But God did give them one command. God told Adam, "You may surely eat of every tree of the garden, but of the tree of the knowledge of good and evil you shall not eat, for in the day that you eat of it you shall surely die" (Genesis 2:16–17).

Have you ever been told not to do something but did it anyway?

> **HAVE YOU EVER BEEN TOLD NOT TO DO SOMETHING BUT DID IT ANYWAY?**

Most of us have disobeyed someone before. We've disobeyed our teachers or parents. Adam and Eve did what you and I probably would have done too. They had all the fruit but were told not to eat from one tree. Just one tree.

So, what happened next?

A serpent slithered its way into the Garden, and it spoke. It lied to Eve and told her God was a liar. But God is perfect—He only does good things and cannot lie. The serpent told her that God didn't really say she would die. The serpent was smart. He knew exactly what to say to confuse and **TEMPT** Eve. He tried to make sin look fun so that Eve would disobey God. So, both Adam and Eve ate from the tree of the knowledge of good and evil. They disobeyed God.

Disobedience has another name. It's called **SIN.** God was not pleased with their disobedience. God gave them the very best and wanted them to have the very best. But even before God told Adam and Eve that they disobeyed, they knew that what they did was wrong.

Sometimes I'll watch funny home videos on TV or on the internet. The best videos are ones with kids in them. I remember a video of a two-year-old boy who was at the dinner table with his family as they were about to eat. The dad was going to pray. As soon as everyone's head was bowed, the boy began to eat his spaghetti. (The boy must have done this often since the dad knew to film it.) The boy had one hand over his eyes and,

with the other hand, he would scoop a big spoonful of spaghetti into his mouth. The dad knew that the boy was eating, but he kept on praying. The boy would look up to see if anyone noticed, and then he would go back to eating.

The boy knew he was disobeying. The dad knew he was disobeying. The funny part was, the boy thought he could hide in plain sight! Adam and Eve did the same thing when they found out God knew they had disobeyed. They hid! They tried to hide behind trees so God couldn't see them. But they couldn't really hide from God.

God created them. He loved them more than they could imagine. And because He loved them, He helped them see how their sin hurt themselves, the Garden, and everything around them. Their disobedience is often called **THE FALL.** This is when sin entered the world. And because they sinned, we sin too.

Sin came into the world, and all of a sudden, Adam and Eve didn't get along like they used to. Giving birth would be painful. Doing work would become hard (think about how hard it can be to do your homework or house chores!). And eventually, every person would die and return to the ground (Genesis 3:16–19).[1]

When sin came into the world, it ruined all the good

things God made. Every person everywhere sins. God does not want us to sin. Like Adam and Eve, our sin is disobedience to God.

THE BIG IDEA
Sin ruined God's creation, and now there are problems with our friendships with one another, but God always had a plan to rescue us.

A really sad part of the fall is that because of sin we sometimes dislike people who are different from us. You and I might sometimes be mean to other people just because they have darker skin or lighter skin. Or because they wear different clothes than we do. Or because they don't sound the way we sound.

Just like we are made in the image of God, we are also made in the image of Adam now too (Genesis 5:3; Romans 5:12).[2] Like Adam, we are sinners.

BECAUSE OF SIN – sometimes we're **UNKIND.**
BECAUSE OF SIN – sometimes we're **HATEFUL.**

BECAUSE OF SIN—sometimes we're **UNFAIR.**

BECAUSE OF SIN—sometimes we're **UNFORGIVING.**

BECAUSE OF SIN—sometimes we **LIE.**

BECAUSE OF SIN—sometimes we **MAKE BAD CHOICES.**

BECAUSE OF SIN—sometimes we **DO BAD THINGS.**

Because of sin—we need **FORGIVENESS.** Have you ever needed to apologize to someone for something you did?

> **HAVE YOU EVER NEEDED TO APOLOGIZE TO SOMEONE FOR SOMETHING YOU DID?**

Maybe you were unkind to a sibling or didn't share. Did you say I'm sorry? Sometimes when we say I'm sorry, the person says "Okay" or "Thank you." And sometimes they say, "I forgive you." We are so thankful for their forgiveness. Well, when we sin, we need forgiveness, and when we say sorry to God, He forgives us.

We need God to wash away our sin. We need to be rescued from our sin. God didn't ignore Adam and Eve's sin. There were consequences for what they did. But God always had a plan to rescue them and rescue us. God sent a person to forgive us and to help us not do those bad things. This person helps us enjoy each other, and most importantly, because of this person we can have a relationship with God! Do you know who that person is?

JESUS SAVES

WHAT DO YOU THINK?

Here are some questions for you to think about. You can write out your answers in a notebook or journal or talk about your answers with others.

1 How would you define sin?

2 Adam and Eve could have ignored the serpent, but they didn't. They decided they wanted to eat the fruit on the tree. Can you think of a time you did something you were told not to do? Why did you do it?

3 Why do you think it's good to obey God?

4 God sent a rescuer. Who do you think He is?

Do you remember the big idea of this chapter? Look back at The Big Idea. Sing it, rap it, or chant it so that you can remember it. Then share it with a friend!

ACTIVITY

We are going to play a memory game. Grab a separate sheet of paper for writing. Write each of the letters of the word "rescuer" on a separate line, like this:

R

E

S

C

U

E

R

Beside each letter, write a word that begins with that letter and best describes our Rescuer. Here's an example using the word "ocean."

OCTOPUS

CORAL REEF

EEL

ALGAE

NARWHAL

Now it's your turn! On your piece of paper, do the same with R E S C U E R.

You can play games like this one to memorize concepts and phrases. Think about other words we've discussed (like *forgiveness*) and write those down too.

CHAPTER 3

OUR WONDERFUL RESCUER

I love giving gifts. I love thinking about what to give for a gift. I love imagining people's faces as they open the gift. There's just something so wonderful about giving gifts. And, of course, I love to get gifts from people as well.

What's the best gift you've ever been given?

WHAT'S THE BEST GIFT YOU'VE EVER BEEN GIVEN?

Gifts are special. But there's one gift that is greater than all gifts. God gave us the gift of His Son, Jesus. He is our best gift ever!

For God loved the world so much that he gave his only Son, so that everyone who believes in him may not die but have eternal life. (John 3:16 GNT)

Earlier, I asked you to name our Rescuer. Did you get it right? Yes, it's Jesus! God loved the world so much. He loved everything that He created. We ruined it, but He always planned to rescue it. And He did! God loved you and me so much that He sent His Son Jesus to be our Rescuer.

The Bible helps us understand that human beings, all of us everywhere, have sinned against God, and there are consequences for that sin. Sin separates us from God. Because of our sin we don't get to be God's friends. Because of our sin we deserve to be taken away from God and His goodness forever.

But God is so loving that He made a way for us to be forgiven of our sin. Our sin is like a muddy, stinky shirt we wear. But when God forgives us of our sin, it's like He takes our muddy, stinky shirt and gives us a brand new, clean, and sparkly shirt. Forgiveness means that God gave us a way to not be punished for our sin. He gave us Jesus.

Jesus lived a perfect life. That means He never, ever, ever sinned. He never disobeyed God. He always chose to love God and to love people. He never made bad choices. Even though He lived a perfect life, Jesus was hung on a cross. A cross was where people who did very bad things were hung to die. But Jesus had never done a bad thing in His whole life. Why did He have to die on the cross?

Have you ever had a substitute teacher? When your regular teacher doesn't come to school, a different teacher takes her place. Well, Jesus became our substitute. When you and I should have been punished for our sin, Jesus took our place instead. Jesus died on the cross so that He could take our sins away. When Jesus died on the cross, He was being punished for our sins so that you and I don't have to be punished for our sins.

But guess what? Jesus did not stay dead! He came back alive three days later. He beat sin and death. At the RESURRECTION—when Jesus came back alive after being dead—He proved that He really is the Son of God, that He really did live a perfect life, and that He really did take the punishment for our sins. He won! That's why we celebrate Easter and often sing, "He is risen!" Jesus is alive and has made a way for you and me to have a relationship with God. This is the GOSPEL or Good News—the good news of what God has done for us through Jesus.

The Good News is good because all the bad things that we have ever done or will ever do have been forgiven by God through Jesus. He forgives us completely. God doesn't hold grudges. He doesn't stay mad at us when we make bad choices. WHEN YOU ASK GOD FOR FORGIVENESS, ALL THE SINFUL THINGS YOU'VE EVER DONE OR SAID GET ERASED IN THE EYES OF GOD. Erased, just as if you had never done those things. It's hard to believe, but it's true. When you ask God to forgive you, He does. He forgives you because Jesus already took the punishment for your sins when He died on the cross.

God sent Jesus to die for people from every nation, every language, and every tribe. Anyone who believes in Jesus can be rescued! We sinned, but God sent His Son to die on the cross and pay the price we could not pay for our sins. Because of Jesus we can love one another. Because of Jesus we can come to God the Father. The gospel is for all nations and all people.

You know how you have to do all your homework to get a good grade? If you don't do your school work, you will likely fail the class. Our relationship with God is NOT like that. You and I don't have to be perfect or "earn a good grade" to be friends with Jesus. We can never be perfect. Only Jesus is perfect. We get to be His friend because He loves us, not because we're good enough.

Even if we have been left out or bullied, Jesus wants to be our friend. Even when others don't treat us how we should be treated, Jesus never treats us that way. Jesus will never be unkind. Jesus always loves.

You and I still sin. When we sin, we can ask God to forgive us. And every day we remember that God forgives us. When God forgives us, we become Christians. That means we become DISCIPLES, or followers, of Jesus.

THE BIG IDEA

God loved the world so much that He sent His son Jesus to rescue it, and now we can have a relationship with God forever.

Here's some more good news. You and I sin, but we are *still* made in the image of God.

GOD IS KIND – WE CAN BE KIND TOO.

GOD IS LOVING – WE CAN BE LOVING TOO.

GOD IS FAIR – WE CAN BE FAIR TOO.

GOD IS FORGIVING – WE CAN BE FORGIVING TOO.

GOD IS TRUTHFUL – WE CAN BE TRUTHFUL TOO.

GOD IS WISE – WE CAN BE WISE TOO.

GOD IS GOOD – WE CAN DO GOOD TOO.

I love hearing about how people learned about Jesus. Have you ever heard about the apostle Paul in the Bible? What happened to Paul is amazing. We first meet Paul (also known as Saul) at the death of Stephen, a friend of Jesus (Acts 7:58).[1] Paul hated Jesus and he hated people who loved Jesus.

Paul went through homes and took innocent men and women to prison. He ordered other people to kill men and women who loved Jesus. He destroyed churches and was happy that people killed and beat followers of Jesus. He was the last person anyone would have thought would become a follower of Jesus Christ too. But God saved Paul. When Paul learned about Jesus, he began telling everyone he knew about the Good News.

Jesus changed everything about Paul. Paul once hated Jesus. Now he wanted to obey Jesus. Paul did terrible things to churches. Now he wanted to help churches grow. Paul would never have talked to others about Jesus. Now that's all he could talk about! His life changed. That's what happens when we give our lives to Jesus. Jesus changes us so that we become more like Him. And that is a very, very good thing.

When we believe in Jesus, the same thing that happened to Paul happens to us. **WE WANT TO OBEY JESUS BECAUSE HE LOVES US AND BECAUSE HE GAVE HIS LIFE FOR US.**

Why is it important for us to learn and understand how Jesus changes everything? As we continue reading, we will learn that Jesus gives us a family: the church. We will learn that Jesus helps us love our family and friends and people we don't even know. We will learn that Jesus helps us become friends with people who are not like us.

Do you know Jesus? Whether you answered yes or no, this week you can ask someone you know more questions about Jesus or you can go through these questions together.

WHAT DO YOU THINK?

Here are some questions for you to think about. You can write out your answers in a notebook or journal or talk about your answers with others.

1 Why do you and I need forgiveness from God?

2 What did Jesus do so that we could receive God's forgiveness?

3 Can you list a few ways that knowing Jesus changes everything?

4 Have you ever been left out or made fun of? How does knowing about Jesus' love for you help you when other people aren't kind to you?

Do you remember the big idea of this chapter? Look back at The Big Idea. Sing it, rap it, or chant it so that you can remember it. Then share it with a friend!

ACTIVITY

We often celebrate Jesus on major holidays like Christmas and Easter, but we can celebrate Jesus all year round. Use the clues below to name a few facts about Jesus from the Bible. Look up the Bible verse given for each clue, then fill in the blanks with your answers. Like a treasure hunt, you can search the Bible too!

Grab a sheet of paper and write your answers there so you can do this activity again.

1   Jesus is the _____ of God. (John 20:31)

2   Because of our sin, we deserve _____, but God gave us the free gift of eternal life through Jesus Christ. (Romans 6:23)

3   Jesus never, ever _____. He lived the perfect life. (Hebrews 4:15)

4   The Good News (the gospel) is that Jesus Christ died for our sins, was buried, and was _____ on the third day. (1 Corinthians 15:3–4)

5   A disciple is someone who _____ Jesus. (Matthew 16:24)

6 Jesus came to rescue all kinds of different people! People from every nation, every tribe, and every _____. (Revelation 7:9–10)

7 Because of Jesus we can _____ one another. (1 John 4:7)

8 When we are honest with God and tell Him how we disobeyed, He promises to _____ us of our sin and make us clean again. (1 John 1:9)

9 When we believe in Jesus, He gives us _____ life. (John 3:16)

10 When we trust in Jesus, God makes us His _____. (John 1:12)

CHAPTER 4

MORE THAN GETTING ALONG

"I love hamburgers!"

"I love my new socks!"

"I love movies!"

You and I love all sorts of things. We use that word "love" a lot. *Love* is a special word, but we often say it about everything we *like*. But the word love is even more special than we could imagine. In the Bible, we learn that love isn't just a word but a word you and I are told to obey. It is a special word indeed!

In the book of Mark in the Bible, we read about a time when

Jesus spoke to a very smart man. We don't know the man's name, but we do know that he was a person who studied the law of God. He is called a scribe, and that means he likely knew the teachings in the first five books of the Bible.

Have you ever met someone who seemed to know everything about a topic? Maybe they are really good at math or always have the right answers about social studies. They are like the man talking to Jesus—he knew a lot about God.

> ## HAVE YOU EVER MET SOMEONE WHO SEEMED TO KNOW EVERYTHING ABOUT A TOPIC?

But he didn't know everything. In fact, he had some important questions. The scribe asked Jesus, "Which commandment is the most important of all?" (Mark 12:28). In God's Word there are many commands. Commands are rules that God gave us so that we can love God and live happy lives. You may have heard of the Ten Commandments. These commands help you and me understand how to follow Jesus. God's commands are good. So, the scribe wanted to know: Out of all the commands in the Old Testament, which one is the most important?

Jesus answered,

"The most important is, 'Hear, O Israel: The Lord our God, the Lord is one. And you shall love the Lord your God with all your heart and with all your soul and with all your mind and with all your strength.'

The second is this: 'You shall love your neighbor as yourself.' There is no other commandment greater than these." (Mark 12:29–31)

There it is. There is that word *love*. Jesus told the scribe that every command is summed up in two commands. That means if you and I obey these two commands, we will obey every other command.

The first commandment is about how we think and feel about God. Have you ever thought about how you think and feel about God? Have you ever told God that you love Him? You and I are told that we are supposed to love God with everything in us. We should love God with all our heart, all our soul, all our mind, and all our strength. This command has been named the **GREAT COMMANDMENT** because it is big and important!

Think of something you really like. Now think about something you love. Do you love God more than that person or thing? Jesus says we should love God more than everything.

> # THINK ABOUT SOMETHING YOU LOVE. DO YOU LOVE GOD MORE THAN THAT PERSON OR THING?

When we love God that much, we will want to obey Him. We won't do this perfectly. Actually, we will need to ask God every day for help to love Him with all our heart, soul, mind, and strength. Even right now, you can ask Him for help. He knows it will be hard for us to love Him more than anything else. He will help us!

We have a helper called the Holy Spirit. The Holy Spirit is God who comes to live inside of us when we trust in Jesus. If your brain is about to explode, no worries, most adults find this to be unbelievable and amazing too! When we ask God for help to love Him and to love other people, it is the Holy Spirit who gives us the strength to love. The Holy Spirit helps us remember God and do good things (John 14:16).[1]

But that is not the end of the commandment. Jesus says that we are supposed to love our neighbor as ourselves. Before we can dive into what that means, we need to figure out who our neighbor is.

Who do you think your neighbor is? Maybe you are thinking about the person who lives next door to you and your family. That's definitely your neighbor. But that's not all. **YOUR NEIGHBOR IS ANYONE YOU TALK TO, SEE, OR INTERACT WITH.** That's a lot of people! Your neighbor includes your classmates, your siblings, the person you may play a game with—even through a virtual game.

Okay, now that we understand that "neighbor" means everyone, think about what Jesus is commanding us to do. Jesus tells us to treat everyone like we would want to be treated. This means that every good thing you want, you are supposed to also want that good thing for your neighbor. Do you want good grades? You should hope that your classmates or siblings or friends also get good grades. Do you want to be happy? You should want everyone around you to be happy too.

These are only a few examples, but there's much more. Think about how you want to be treated. What about how you want others to think about you?

> **THINK ABOUT HOW YOU WANT TO BE TREATED. WHAT ABOUT HOW YOU WANT OTHERS TO THINK ABOUT YOU?**

That's the kind of love Jesus is talking about. He wants us to think of people as greater than ourselves. Jesus wants us to be patient, kind, forgiving, and honest with others (1 Corinthians 13:4–7).[2]

THE BIG IDEA

God commands us to love Him with all our heart, soul, mind, and strength and to love our neighbor—no matter who it is—as ourselves.

You might already be thinking, *Boy, this is hard.* But there's more! God commands us to a radical love for *others.* I remember one day when someone called me a mean name. I wanted to say something mean back, but the Holy Spirit helped me remember that I needed to love this person. I thought to myself, *This is hard—it's an extremely hard command.* That's what makes it radical. So radical it includes loving people who hate us (Matthew 5:43–48)[3] and loving without expecting anything back from people (Luke 6:27–36).[4]

Just like how we should love God, loving the way Jesus tells us to love others is impossible if we try to do it without help. You can ask your parent or guardian for help to love better. Maybe you have an older friend or pastor you can ask to help you. But most of all, God tells us in

His Word that we can ask Him for help to obey His commandment to love (Hebrews 4:14–16).[5] You and I can and should ask Jesus to help us love our neighbor.

You might also be thinking, *Wait, I thought this was about learning about people who look different than me?* Yes! God's commandment to love our neighbor means that we should love those who look different than us. That doesn't mean we ignore their differences. It means that if we love them, we can learn to enjoy their differences (I'll share more about this in the next chapter).

The really good news is that we love others because God first loved us (1 John 4:10).[6] The gospel that I explained in chapter 3 is for every person in the world. It is where God chooses to show us His amazing love. God loved the world and gave His Son to save the world. Knowing how much God loves us makes us brave enough to love others, even when they are different from us.

As Christians, we aren't just supposed to get along with one another. It's important to get along, no doubt about it. But what God really wants is for us to have our hearts and minds so changed by Him that we can't help but love everyone around us. **EVERY WORD WE SAY AND EVERYTHING WE DO SHOULD BE ABOUT SHOWING EACH PERSON THEY ARE LOVED.**

I don't know anyone in the whole world who has ever loved perfectly. You have probably been unkind to someone. Maybe you ignored them. Maybe you made fun of someone. I definitely have not loved perfectly either! You and I need the same thing—forgiveness. God forgives us of every unloving thought and every unloving act we've ever done. Right now, you can ask Him to forgive you and help you love better today and every day.

WHAT DO YOU THINK?

Here are some questions for you to think about. You can write out your answers in a notebook or journal or talk about your answers with others.

1 What does it mean to love your neighbor as yourself? Does that sound easy or hard to do?

2 What are three ways you can show your friends that you love them? (For example: Write a friend a card thanking them for being a good friend.)

3 Why do you think it is important to love those who do not look or sound like you? What are ways you can show them love? (For example: Get to know them. Sit next to them at lunch so they are not alone. Stand up for them if someone is making fun of them.)

4 Can you think of a way you have not loved others well? God tells us we can go to Him for help.

Do you remember the big idea of this chapter? Look back at The Big Idea. Sing it, rap it, or chant it so that you can remember it. Then share it with a friend!

ACTIVITY

Can you think of a way you have not loved others well? God tells us we can go to Him for help. Sometimes it helps to write out a prayer to God. Write out a prayer in a notebook or journal asking God for His help so that you can love other people better. Remember: God loves to help us do that! Now, find a Bible and read Hebrews 4:16.

CHAPTER 5

A SURPRISING, COLORFUL FAMILY

Let's do a quick review of the great news we've learned about so far. We have learned that God created everything and He made people in His image. We were created to reflect what God is like by loving Him and loving others. We get to have a relationship with God and forgiveness for our sins because Jesus died on the cross and came back alive on the third day. Isn't all that we have learned awesome? God is good and kind to us!

Each time I share some good news with you, I get to share even more good news! What God has done gets better and better the more we learn. What has been exciting for you to learn so far?

WHAT HAS BEEN EXCITING FOR YOU TO LEARN SO FAR?

Here's some more good news. Did you know that you have a colorful family?

For some of you, your brothers and sisters are from different parts of the world. You may have a brother or sister or cousin or aunt or uncle who has curly hair or straight hair or brown skin or pink skin. You may have a parent from another country or one who has skin that looks different from yours. For many of you, your family *is* colorful.

But I have a surprise for you. Every one of us who knows and loves Jesus is a part of a big, massive, enormous, delightfully colorful family. **OUR FAMILY IS CALLED THE FAMILY OF GOD.** It is a special family designed only for those who know Jesus. Everyone who believes in Jesus has been adopted into God's family. God is our heavenly Father and we are His children (John 1:12–13).[1]

People all over the world are a part of God's family. It is one big family, and all are welcomed to be a part of it because of what Jesus did for us. Once we have trusted in Jesus, we are all counted as God's children. This means that we are all brothers and sisters in Christ! The family of God is important and special. It's so important that Jesus gave His life for this family and now allows us to be His brothers and sisters (Romans 8:16–17).[2] Amazing!

Did you know you are a part of a generation? You might be a part of the generation called Generation Alpha or the one called Generation Z. Generations started at the beginning of time and span all of history. There were many generations before you and there will be many generations after you. That means our Christian family reaches back generations and is from all over the world. Now that's a big, BIG family!

God doesn't choose His children because of how they look. He doesn't say you must be tall, light-skinned, blonde, or green-eyed to be part of His family. Your church family may not look like you or sound like you, but that is a part of God's perfect design. We have a delightfully different family on purpose. It was God's idea to make people different and to bring us together in a family. And you can enjoy loving your church family and thank God for each person.

One day I was teaching a Sunday school class for kindergarten kids. I let them know that they are made in the image of God. I told them about all that Jesus did so that they could have a relationship with Him. They were so excited when I told them that they weren't only friends— they are brothers and sisters. My daughter, Sydney, was in the class and wrapped her arms around one of her friends.

When that friend got home, she told her mom, "Sydney is not just my friend, she's my sister!"

Those little kindergarteners were so excited, and we should be too!

THE BIG IDEA
God has given us a delightfully different, totally unique, and absolutely colorful family called the church.

Do you remember the story about the apostle Paul and how much he hated the church? And remember how Jesus changed his heart and mind? After Paul became a Christian, he couldn't stop speaking about Jesus. I'd like to tell you about my story too!

I learned about the Lord at a young age like you, but it wasn't until a friend told me more about Jesus that I trusted in Him. My friend and I were very different. She had light skin, and I have dark skin. She lived in a large home, and I lived in a small home. I was in college, and she decided not to go to school. We were very different. But it didn't matter. She loved Jesus and wanted to make sure I could know and love Him too.

We became friends, and then we became sisters in Christ. Just like the kids in that kindergarten class, I was so excited! But the Lord didn't stop giving me new friends who were not like me. I had a friend who loved to dress in cowboy hats and another friend who dressed fancy for work. I had a friend from China and a friend from Ethiopia. We were all very different! But our love for one another helped other people learn about Jesus too.

Jesus said, "By [your love for each other] all people will know that you are my disciples, if you have love for one another" (John 13:35).

The way we treat our brothers and sisters is important. **JESUS COMMANDED US TO LOVE GOD WITH ALL OUR HEARTS, SOULS, MINDS, AND STRENGTH AND TO LOVE OUR NEIGHBOR AS OURSELVES.** And our love for our brothers and sisters in the church signals to people who do not know Jesus that we are His friends.

For example, a stop sign signals (or tells) you to stop. When you see those red, octagonal-shaped signs with the big white letters STOP, you stop. When people who know Jesus act in a way that is patient, kind, and loving toward one another, it signals that Jesus has made them to be like a family. We know that we *are* a family.

Let me make sure you understand. I am not saying we should leave our families for our brothers and sisters in Christ. My three sisters growing up were my best friends. God graciously placed me into a family, and we love each other dearly. My point is that the family of God is important. It's so important that Jesus gave His life for this family, and He gives us a special gift—brothers and sisters in our church. Amazing!

God has a colorful family, and that means we do too!

WHAT DO YOU THINK?

Here are some questions for you to think about. You can write out your answers in a notebook or journal or talk about your answers with others.

1 How does it make you feel to think of your church as a family?

2 God is our Father, and we are His children. Why is it special that we are children of God?

3 Why do you think it's important to know that God made a family with people from every country and every language? Why is it important to know that this is your family too?

4 Why should we love our church family?

Do you remember the big idea of this chapter? Look back at The Big Idea. Sing it, rap it, or chant it so that you can remember it. Then share it with a friend!

ACTIVITY

Treasure Hunt: Go outside and try to find ten different objects. (If you can't go outside, that's okay! Find ten different objects in your home.) Once you have your items, fill out the chart below. Notice how God made each thing very different, but each thing is a part of God's creation. That's like the church. God made a family filled with people who are different in many ways, but He is the Father of us all. God made us delightfully different!

TREASURE HUNT

OBJECT	COLOR	SHAPE	TEXTURE (smooth, rough, prickly?)	SIZE	HEAVY or LIGHT?
1					
2					
3					
4					
5					
6					
7					
8					
9					
10					

CHAPTER 6

WE ARE DIFFERENT; WE ARE ALSO THE SAME

My kids are artistic. I bet some of you are too. They like to draw and paint. They are creative and have great imaginations. They get their brilliant, artistic minds from the Lord and from their dad . . . not so much from me. In fact, I'm the complete opposite. While I'm creative, I'm not at all artistic and my imagination isn't very, well, imaginative.

I remember one day when my son was four years old and he put his little hand on mine and began to pray, "Lord, make mommy's hands be able to draw." It was a sweet prayer. When he was finished, I looked at him and simply said, "God may never make mommy's hands able to draw. But He has given me other gifts for His glory." My son didn't get it then, but thankfully he now understands the unique ways that God has gifted each of us.

God's creation is so diverse. God could have made us all the exact same, but He didn't. And our differences are good. The Bible tells us that our differences help each other.

The apostle Paul, the same one we learned about before, wrote a letter to the church in a city called Corinth. That letter is now called Corinthians in the Bible. In that letter, Paul shared that the church is like a body with many parts (1 Corinthians 12:12).[1]

Think about the human body. We have arms, legs, eyes, a nose, a head, ears, and all sorts of body parts to make up one body. And each body part does something different. Our eyes are not like our mouth. Our feet are not like our elbows. Our nose is not like our knees. And that's a good thing! Can you imagine how silly you would look if your whole body was made up of just one body part, like the ear? Thankfully, God gave us different body parts that each do different things.

The church is the same way. The church is made up of many people, and these people are not all the same. The church is made up of people with all kinds of different gifts. Some people can sing. Some people love leading. Some enjoy teaching. Some people like making meals for others. Some people love to help. God is so creative that we can't even list all the different ways He has made us!

Can you think of ways God has made you? What are things that you like to do? God created you like that!

> ## CAN YOU THINK OF WAYS GOD HAS MADE YOU? WHAT ARE THINGS THAT YOU LIKE TO DO?

God's family isn't only diverse because of the different ways we look and speak; we are also different in what we like to do and in the SPIRITUAL GIFTS God has given us. Do you see how wonderful our differences are? We can celebrate how God has made us.

But we have a problem.

We don't always get along. **OUR DIFFERENCES AREN'T SINFUL, BUT THE WAY WE TREAT EACH OTHER BECAUSE OF OUR DIFFERENCES CAN BE.** Because of sin we sometimes dislike a person simply because of the color of their skin. Because of sin we are sometimes jealous of people who have gifts and talents that are not like ours. Because of sin we may play favorites with people. When we play favorites with other people, this is called the sin of partiality. **PARTIALITY** is sinful favoritism. It means leaving others out or ignoring them because of your favoritism. Because favoritism can be a big problem in our friendships, let's spend more time thinking about it.

We can play favorites for many reasons. One that stands out in the Bible in the book of James is favoritism for the rich. James was not happy with the people he was writing to because they were playing favorites. At their church, they were putting the poor people in the back and letting the rich people sit in the front. They were showing favoritism.

Let's look at James 2:1–4, 8–9:

My dear brothers and sisters, how can you claim to have faith in our glorious Lord Jesus Christ if you favor some people over others?

For example, suppose someone comes into your meeting dressed in fancy clothes and expensive jewelry, and another comes in who is poor and dressed in dirty clothes. If you give special attention and a good seat to the rich person, but you say to the poor one, "You can stand over there, or else sit on the floor"—well, doesn't this discrimination show that your judgments are guided by evil motives?

[. . .]

Yes indeed, it is good when you obey the royal law as found in the Scriptures: "Love your neighbor as yourself." But if you favor some people over others, you are committing a sin. You are guilty of breaking the law. (NLT)

What words did James use to remind them not to play favorites? He reminded them of the Great Commandment. He reminded them to love their neighbor. One reason that we shouldn't show favoritism is because it is not loving.

You know who doesn't ever show favoritism? God!

For God does not show favoritism.
(Romans 2:11 NIV)

Because we are made in the image of God, we can be fair, we can be loving, and we should not show favoritism. What are some ways we sometimes show favoritism?

1   Leaving someone out of a game to seem cool to our friends.

2   Sitting with certain people at lunch and leaving out others.

3   Not speaking to certain people because of how they look.

I am not saying that we can't have good friends. We can have good friends. I have a few friends I'd call my best friends. We can hang out with those good friends. We can spend a lot of time with those friends. The only time our friendships are a problem is if we leave people out because we don't like that they are different from us. That is partiality. We would be so sad if someone didn't include us. And aren't we so happy God includes us in His family and that He doesn't have favorites? We are all God's favorites!

So, we've named a few reasons why we shouldn't play favorites: 1) We want to love those who are not like us, and 2) God doesn't have favorites.

THE BIG IDEA

We sometimes mistreat each other because of our differences, and this is sinful. We can ask God to help us treat people the way we want to be treated, even when they are different from us.

We've talked about how God made us all different. But did you know that we are also the same?

We are much more the same than we are different.

We are all made in the image of God.

We all sin.

We all need forgiveness.

Jesus forgives all who ask Him.

God the Father is the Father of all people who know Jesus.

Everyone who knows and loves Jesus is our brother and sister.

We all have different gifts and talents that God gives us.

We are all created by God, made in the image of God, and rescued by Jesus. We are the same! Sin confuses us and makes us forget how we are beautifully different and wonderfully the same.

This is another reason why it's so silly to be unkind to

other people—they are more like us than they are different. We are all equal. We are all people.

I haven't always been fair to everyone around me. I've shown favoritism before. When I've done this, I've asked the Lord to forgive me and to help me do better the next time. If you have shown favoritism to certain people or been unkind to those who do not look like you, you can ask God for forgiveness too.

And I know what it feels like to be left out. It doesn't feel good. But God never excludes anyone. God doesn't show favoritism. **YOU AND I CAN BE HAPPY KNOWING THAT GOD LOVES US.**

WHAT DO YOU THINK?

Here are some questions for you to think about. You can write out your answers in a notebook or journal or talk about your answers with others.

1 Think of someone who is very different from you. List five to ten ways this person is the same as you (similar to you).

2 Think of someone you have treated unfairly because they were different from you. Then ask God for forgiveness.

3 You might need to ask for forgiveness, and you might need to forgive someone else. What has God given you to help you forgive and ask forgiveness?

 Do you remember the big idea of this chapter? Look back at The Big Idea. Sing it, rap it, or chant it so that you can remember it. Then share it with a friend!

ACTIVITY

Creative God, Colorful Us
Sugar Cookie Recipe

2 ¾ cups all-purpose flour
1 teaspoon baking soda
½ teaspoon baking powder
1 cup butter, softened
1 ½ cups white sugar

1 egg
1 teaspoon vanilla extract (or your favorite flavor
such as peppermint or orange)
Rainbow Sprinkles

To make delicious cookies, you have to use different ingredients. In the same way, God has made a colorful and delightfully different family called the church. Even though the recipe ingredients are all different, they come together to make one cookie. In the same way, God's children are all different, but we are all the same because we are all forgiven and loved by God. Together, we are one big family of God. Now that's sweet!

Ask a parent or guardian to help you make your sugar cookies. Here's how you do it:

LET'S COOK

Ask a parent or guardian to do this first:

Preheat oven to 375 degrees F (190 degrees C). In a small bowl, stir together flour, baking soda, and baking powder. Set aside.

Now do this:

In a large bowl, mix the softened butter and sugar with an electric mixer (if available) until as smooth as possible. Beat in egg and vanilla. Gradually stir in the dry ingredients. Roll rounded teaspoonfuls of dough into balls, dip balls of dough into the sprinkles, and place onto ungreased cookie sheets.

Almost done:

Bake 8 to 10 minutes in the preheated oven, or to the color of your liking (golden or light brown). Let cookies rest on the cookie sheet two minutes, then move to wire racks to cool. Eat up!

CHAPTER 7

OUR FOREVER FRIENDS

Do you have a BFF? When I was younger, my friends and I would label each other BFF, which means best friends forever. Boys don't often call their buds BFFs, but some of you probably have a buddy that you consider your "best" buddy.

One of the hard parts about getting older is that sometimes those friends who were your BFFs are no longer your friends when you get older. Sometimes friends move to different schools. Sometimes friends move to different cities or states. Sometimes friends disagree and decide to no longer be friends. Or sometimes we simply grow up and change. There are many reasons best friends sometimes don't last forever. At least not in our lifetime on earth.

Do you remember how Adam and Eve sinned, but that wasn't the end of the story? Remember that? There was more. Much more. So much more. God had a plan to rescue all that was destroyed by sin. He sent His Son, Jesus. Jesus is our Rescuer. But guess what? That's not the end of the story! There's even good news about our BFFs. If we know Jesus, we will spend eternity (that's forever!) worshiping Him and enjoying our friends. Forever!

When we die, we go to be with the Lord. The Bible tells us that God is preparing a house with many rooms for us (John 14:2)![1] Think of the most beautiful house you've ever seen. What was it like?

THINK OF THE MOST BEAUTIFUL HOUSE YOU'VE EVER SEEN. WHAT WAS IT LIKE?

God's house will be more beautiful than anything you could ever imagine. And it will have everything you need:

food, water, you name it. That sounds pretty great, but there's something even better than that.

When we die and go to be with Jesus, the Bible tells us that we will be perfect. Everyone who knows Jesus will never sin again! We will never get angry. We will never be mean. We will never show favoritism. And no one will be angry with us. No one will be mean to us. No one will leave us out. We will enjoy one another forever and always.

Can you imagine how wonderful it will be to be perfect? Can you imagine a place where there are no wars and fights? That's the difference between heaven and earth. A recent trip to a zoo reminded me of that difference.

There's a safari zoo in a small town not too far from my own. Zebras, ostriches, antelope, emus, and even giraffes roam around a large area of the zoo while visitors slowly drive through the area. Although we had to stay in our car, we were allowed to roll down our windows and feed the animals. The ostriches have figured out that people drive through the park with food and don't hesitate to force their heads into your car! They want the food. But even though they usually are harmless, it can be scary the first time you feed one. Let's just say, my daughter hasn't asked us to go again!

Read this beautiful picture of Heaven from the book of Isaiah in the Bible:

In that day the wolf and the lamb
    will live together;
    the leopard will lie down
        with the baby goat.
The calf and the yearling will be safe with the lion,
    and a little child will lead them all.
The cow will graze near the bear.
    The cub and the calf will lie down together.
    The lion will eat hay like a cow.
The baby will play safely near the hole of a cobra.
    Yes, a little child will put its hand in a nest of
        deadly snakes without harm.
Nothing will hurt or destroy in all my holy mountain,
    for as the waters fill the sea,
    so the earth will be filled with people who know
        the LORD.
(11:6–9 NLT)

A baby and a cobra snake playing together! That's pretty incredible. Everything will be perfect. There will be peace and joy and love and laughter—all day, every day.

God is making all things new. That means He is creating a new heaven and new earth.

Revelation 21 gives us a picture of what we can expect there:

Then I saw a new heaven and a new earth, for the first heaven and the first earth had passed away, and the sea was no more. And I saw the holy city, new Jerusalem, coming down out of heaven from God, prepared as a bride adorned for her husband. And I heard a loud voice from the throne saying, "Behold, the dwelling place of God is with man. He will dwell with them, and they will be his people, and God himself will be with them as their God. He will wipe away every tear from their eyes, and death shall be no more, neither shall there be mourning, nor crying, nor pain anymore, for the former things have passed away." (vv. 1–4)

Can you see all the things that will be made new and perfect again? Here's a list to help us see all that God will do:

We will never sin again.

There will be no evil to be found anywhere.

We will never worry about anything.

There will be no more sickness.

There will be no more tears.

No one will ever die again.

The *best* part of heaven will be seeing Jesus face to face (Revelation 22:4).[2] We will thank Him for everything. We will get on our knees and bow down as we **WORSHIP** Him. Jesus prayed that we could get to experience all of these things: "Father, I desire that they also, whom you have given me, may be with me where I am, to see my glory that you have given me because you loved me before the foundation of the world" (John 17:24).

THE BIG IDEA

Every tribe, tongue, language, and nation will be in heaven together perfectly worshiping, loving, and enjoying one another.

God gives us many clues in the Bible for how awesome it will be in heaven. But He also tells us who we'll be there with.

I looked, and there before me was a great multitude that no one could count, from every nation, tribe, people and language, standing before the throne and before the Lamb. (Revelation 7:9 NIV)

Remember how Jesus died for anyone who would believe, for anyone who ever lived, no matter the color of their skin? Jesus made it possible for every tribe, tongue, people, and language to enjoy worshiping God together in heaven.

People from China will be in heaven worshiping God. People from Cambodia will be in heaven worshiping God. People from Ethiopia, Russia, Argentina, the United States, New Zealand, England, and Guatemala will be in heaven, sinless, and together worshiping God. People from every continent will be there.

It was God's idea that heaven would be a place filled with diversity and beauty. If God thought being different from one another was bad, He would not have decided that our differences would follow us straight to heaven. Difference is good. So good that although we will be the same in heaven, we will also be different.

Why do you think it is important to understand what heaven will look like?

WHY DO YOU THINK IT IS IMPORTANT TO UNDERSTAND WHAT HEAVEN WILL LOOK LIKE?

If we understand that God's diverse creation will be in heaven, then it should motivate us to love one another on earth. We will be together—forever. **HEAVEN WILL BE FILLED WITH OLD AND NEW BFFS.** People who once hated each other on earth before Jesus changed them will love one another perfectly in heaven. We will live there together—always happy!

But we don't need to wait until heaven to love and enjoy those not like us. And that is the message of this book. Right now you can begin doing the things you will be doing for eternity in heaven.

RIGHT NOW, YOU CAN ...

Get to know people who do not look like you.

Get to know people who do not speak like you.

Get to know people who have different physical abilities than you.

Be kind to people who do not look like you.

Be kind to people who do not speak like you.

Be kind to people who have different physical abilities than you.

RIGHT NOW, YOU CAN . . .

Invite someone to play who does not look like you.

Invite someone to play who does not speak like you.

Invite someone to play who has a different physical ability than you.

Read about people who do not look like you.

Read about people who do not speak like you.

Read about people who have different physical abilities than you.

There's so much you and I can do right now to help us love and enjoy people not like us, just like we will do in heaven.

WHAT DO YOU THINK?

Here are some questions for you to think about. You can write out your answers in a notebook or journal or talk about your answers with others.

1 Where can we learn about heaven and what it will look like? Why is it important for us to understand what heaven will look like?

2 How does understanding what heaven will look like help you treat people?

3 What is one thing you can do right now to get to know someone not like you?

ACTIVITY

Get out a piece of paper. Draw as many different people as you can. You might need to ask a parent or guardian to help you search for different people in a book or on a computer.

Here are some ideas for what the people could be doing together:

Draw the different people around a table, enjoying eating a dinner together.

Draw the different people in a church building worshiping God together.

Draw the different people in a classroom listening to a teacher together.

Draw the different people on a playground together.

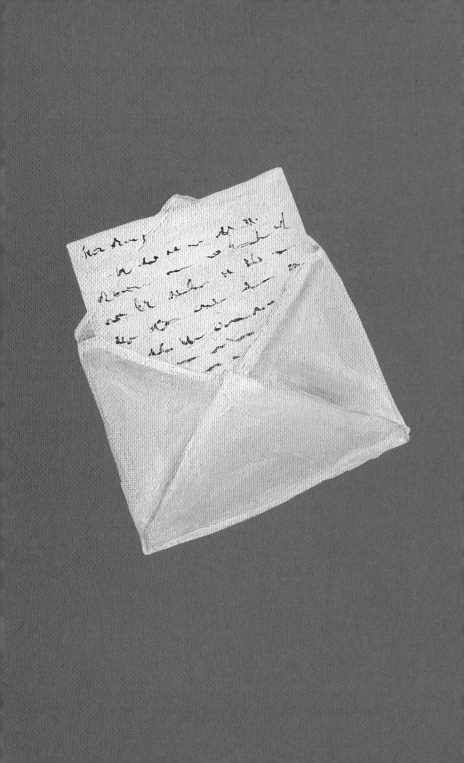

LET'S TALK: WHERE DO WE GO FROM HERE?

Hello again!

I don't know about you, but I love mail! These days, most mail comes in the form of emails on the computer. But once in a while, I'll receive a special note in the mailbox outside my home. I love those mail days! Although this final note isn't coming to you in the mail, I do consider it my special little note to you, my reader and new friend.

We've covered a lot in this book, haven't we? I'm going to give you a tip that might help you for the rest of your life. Everything that you have read in this book will take a lifetime to learn. Yep. You read that right. You and I will spend our entire lives asking God to help us love people the way He has commanded us to. And that's okay, as long as we keep on asking God for help!

Maybe you will remember something in this book when you go to school. Maybe next time you see someone making fun of someone else, you'll know what to think and what to do. Maybe when you see someone who doesn't look like you, you'll be excited to get to know them. Maybe you won't leave people out anymore. And maybe when people leave you out, you'll remember that you are made in the image of God and God loves you.

There's so much that I hope God will do! What are things you hope God will do?

WHAT ARE THINGS YOU HOPE GOD WILL DO?

Because you and I will spend a lifetime learning how to love God and love people, I hope that this book will be the first of many you explore about this very important topic. But keep it close by so you can look at it again. If you have questions about anything you've read, write them down and find a parent or guardian and share your questions. Questions are good! That's how we learn.

And as much as this book is meant to be read, it's also meant to be applied. That means many of the things you've read should lead you to do something. For example, in chapter 7, I suggested you find someone who is not like you and ask them to play. That is one way to apply what you learned about loving others and enjoying people who we will enjoy in heaven.

Now our time has come to an end. I'm smiling big thinking about you and how you are going to love all the different people around you just like Jesus loves us.

Thank you for reading *Creative God, Colorful Us*!

Trillia

HELPFUL WORDS TO KNOW

DISCIPLES: A disciple is a follower of Jesus. A disciple of Jesus believes in and follows His teachings in the Bible.

DIVERSE: If something is diverse, it has a great deal of variety or is very different.

FORGIVENESS: There are different types of forgiveness. This is the definition for the forgiveness of sin. Part of the gospel or Good News is that God counts the good character of Jesus as if it is our good character. He pardons our sin.

GOSPEL or GOOD NEWS: The Bible says, "For all have sinned and fall short of the glory of God" (Romans 3:23). God is perfect but we sin, and our sin separates us from God.

But God's love is so amazing, He sent His Son Jesus so that we would no longer be separated from Him. Jesus lived a perfect life, but when the time came, He died on the cross and rose from the grave. Jesus paid for our sins—He took all the consequences. Because of what He did, we can now have a relationship with God—our sins are forgiven.

When you accept Jesus' free gift of forgiveness, you join His family. The Bible says, "But to all who did receive him, who believed in his name, he gave the right to become children of God" (John 1:12).

The gospel *is* good news!

IMAGE OF GOD: Genesis 1:26–27 tells us that God created humankind as male and female in His image or likeness. We reflect God's image through our character and how we relate to each other and the earth. Because God does something, we should do the same. He takes care of the earth and so should we. He is kind and loving; we can be kind and loving.

PARTIALITY (SINFUL FAVORITISM): The sin of partiality or favoritism is an unfair favoring of one thing or person compared with another.

RESURRECTION: After the death of Jesus on the cross, He was placed in a tomb. On the third day, Jesus rose from the grave and defeated death. Jesus is alive right now at the right hand of God. His resurrection means we, too, will live forever with Him. Jesus lives. He is risen, indeed.

SIN: Sin is the rebellion against God and what He tells us in the Bible, His Word. It's the bad things we do and think that separate us from God.

SPIRITUAL GIFTS: Every person who knows Jesus has been given various characteristics or gifts that are meant to be used for the benefit of others.

TEMPT AND TEMPTATION: Tempt is when someone or something tries to get you to do something wrong or unwise. Temptation is the desire to do something wrong or unwise.

THE FALL: A term describing when Adam and Eve sinned against God and sin and misery entered the whole world.

THE GREAT COMMANDMENT: Jesus summed up the Old Testament law with these words: "'Love the Lord your God with all your heart and with all your soul and with all your mind.' This is the first and greatest commandment. And the second is like it: 'Love your neighbor as yourself.' All the Law and the Prophets hang on these two commandments" (Matthew 22:36–40 NIV). God's command to us is to love Him and love our neighbor. If we do these things, we will be obeying God.

WORSHIP: Worship has many different meanings. The one we use refers to our worship of God as it relates to our love for God. Worship is having a deep respect or reverence for God, and this respect leads to feelings and expressions of love

A LETTER TO THE ADULTS—4 REASONS TO ENJOY OUR DIFFERENCES

Dear Parent or Guardian:

If your child has this book, there's a good chance that you gave it to them. Thank you! I hope that they've enjoyed learning about the Good News and all that God has done through Jesus. One of the many things I've heard from parents in regard to race and ethnicity is that we are all the same and therefore we should be colorblind. Since this book is about how the gospel allows us to enjoy people from every tribe, tongue, and nation and to celebrate difference, I'm sharing reasons why it's important for us to teach our children *not* to be colorblind and how we, too, can enjoy difference.

Can you imagine wanting to be colorblind? And yet I hear that all the time. When I speak with adults about ethnic and racial diversity, it's not long before someone says: "I don't see color. I'm colorblind! My parents taught me not to see color."

This phrase is a way of expressing that all people are seen as just that—people. I've also heard colorblindness cited as a defense against racism, "I'm not racist. I love all people. Actually, I'm colorblind."

But I disagree.

Although people confidently make the claim, I'd like to suggest that we are not colorblind, we don't need to be colorblind, and we actually should strive to *not* be colorblind, because it leads us in the wrong direction. Instead, I want to encourage us to be *colorsmart*. Here's why*. . .

1. BEING COLORBLIND ISN'T REALISTIC.

I'm a Black woman. I cannot—and have no desire to—erase the fact that I am how God made me. There is no hiding my milky-brown, freckled skin. I am who I am. When I walk into a room and I am the only Black woman,

---

* Trillia Newbell, "Helping Your Children See," *Trillia Newbell* (blog), August 10, 2017, http://www.trillianewbell.com/2017/08/10/helping-children-see./.

it's obvious. There's no benefit in pretending. I know it; you know it; we all know it. It's ridiculous to pretend otherwise.

What I'm *not* saying, however, is that we need to act awkward around each other. If we've embraced the fact that God has created us as equals, there's no need or reason for that awkwardness. If someone who is culturally or ethnically different from you comes around, it is unrealistic, unhelpful, and possibly unloving to pretend that you don't notice. So, when your child says, "Mommy, why is that woman wearing a dot on her forehead?" instead of being embarrassed and asking them to be quiet, the *colorsmart* approach is to take that question as an opportunity to positively explain her different, unique culture.

Instead of pretending we are *colorblind*, let's celebrate God's creation and be *colorsmart*.

2. COLORBLINDNESS MISSES THE OPPORTUNITY TO CELEBRATE GOD'S GOOD DESIGN.

Being colorblind seeks to ignore or flatten the differences between us. But being colorsmart enables us to see people as made in the image of God just as we are—acknowledging the beauty of our differences. As God's image bearers, we all have similarities. God doesn't discriminate against certain people groups in His design. We are all equally created to reflect aspects of our Creator God. However, God does create each and every one of us uniquely. This can be acknowledged and celebrated rather than ignored out of fear.

We are not all the same in regard to skin color, interests, likes, gifts, and desires. God has created us different for a purpose, namely His glory. So, instead of striving to be colorblind, let's be colorsmart—recognizing these differences in ways that express genuine interest in and love for our neighbor and being thankful for the beauty of God's amazing design.

Don't we want our kids to also celebrate who they are

as designed by God? We want children to celebrate that God created them and celebrate that God created all people. That is the beautiful reality of creation.

3. THE GOSPEL IS FOR ALL NATIONS.

The most important reason to be colorsmart is that the gospel is for all nations. God celebrates His creation and redemption of all people. The Bible tells us that we sinned, putting everything out of order—part of which is the tragic racial division and hatred we see throughout history. But Scripture shows us how our God is working toward the redemption of *all people* through Christ. And He is glorified now when His people from all nations worship Him together. We can see the fulfillment of His promise to redeem

every tribe, tongue, and nation when we gather, fellowship, and worship with those who are different from us.

4. WE WILL REJOICE IN COLOR FOREVER.

God doesn't erase our distinctions in Scripture, and it is the ultimate reality of our life in eternity. Revelation 5 shows us a beautiful picture of every color, tribe, tongue and nation worshiping *together* in eternity. It is the work of the Lord to reconcile all things—first in reconciling us to Himself, then each of us to one another. We will spend eternity in a New Creation filled—gloriously!—with people of all colors.

So, instead of pretending like we are *colorblind*, let's celebrate God's creation and be *colorsmart*. Like His glorious vision of the last day, let's see the beauty of His people who He has created uniquely. Instead of pretending there are no differences, let's get to know one another. The pursuit of ethnic harmony doesn't require us to ignore how God uniquely designed us. When we celebrate our differences, I believe we reflect what God has demonstrated in His Word. Our children are watching and learning from us, and they can grow to love the nations and to reach out to them with the gospel of grace as we embrace our God-given differences.

BIBLE VERSES FOR YOU TO READ

INTRODUCTION

1. (**2 Timothy 3:16–17**) All Scripture is breathed out by God and profitable for teaching, for reproof, for correction, and for training in righteousness, that the man of God may be complete, equipped for every good work.

CHAPTER 1

1. (**Genesis 1:10, 18, 25**) God called the dry land Earth, and the waters that were gathered together he called Seas. And God saw that it was good. (10)

. . . to rule over the day and over the night, and to separate the light from the darkness. And God saw that it was good. (18)

And God made the beasts of the earth according to their kinds and the livestock according to their kinds, and everything that creeps on the ground according to its kind. And God saw that it was good. (25)

2. **(Genesis 2:5)** When no bush of the field was yet in the land and no small plant of the field had yet sprung up—for the LORD God had not caused it to rain on the land, and there was no man to work the ground.

3. **(Psalm 139:14)** I praise you, for I am fearfully and wonderfully made. Wonderful are your works; my soul knows it very well.

CHAPTER 2

1. **(Genesis 3:16–19)** To the woman he said, "I will surely multiply your pain in childbearing; in pain you shall bring forth children. Your desire shall be contrary to your husband, but he shall rule over you." And to Adam he said, "Because you have listened to the voice of your wife and have eaten of the tree of which I commanded you, 'You shall not eat of it,' cursed is the ground because of you; in pain you shall eat of it all the days of your life; thorns and thistles it shall bring forth for you; and you shall eat the plants of the field. By the sweat of your face you shall eat bread, till you return to the ground, for out of it you were taken; for you are dust, and to dust you shall return."

2. **(Genesis 5:3; Romans 5:12)** When Adam had lived 130 years, he fathered a son in his own likeness, after his image, and named him Seth. (Gen. 5:3)

Therefore, just as sin came into the world through one man, and death through sin, and so death spread to all men because all sinned. (Rom. 5:12)

CHAPTER 3

1. **(Acts 7:58)** Then they cast him out of the city and stoned him. And the witnesses laid down their garments at the feet of a young man named Saul.

CHAPTER 4

1. **(John 14:16)** "And I will ask the Father, and he will give you another Helper, to be with you forever."

2. **(1 Corinthians 13:4–7)** Love is patient and kind; love does not envy or boast; it is not arrogant or rude. It does not insist on its own way; it is not irritable or resentful; it does not rejoice at wrongdoing, but rejoices with the truth. Love bears all things, believes all things, hopes all things, endures all things.

3. **(Matthew 5:43–48)** "You have heard that it was said, 'You shall love your neighbor and hate your enemy.' But I say to you, Love your enemies and pray for those who persecute you, so that you may be sons of your Father who is in heaven. For he makes his sun rise on the evil and on the good, and sends rain on the just and on the unjust. For if you love those who love you, what reward do you have? Do not even the tax collectors do the same? And if you greet only your brothers, what more are you doing than others? Do not even the Gentiles do the same? You therefore must be perfect, as your heavenly Father is perfect."

4. **(Luke 6:27–36)** "But I say to you who hear, Love your enemies, do good to those who hate you, bless those who curse you, pray for those who abuse you. To one who strikes you on the cheek, offer the other also, and from one who takes away your cloak do not withhold your tunic either. Give to everyone who begs from you, and from one who takes away your goods do not demand them back. And as you wish that others would do to you, do so to them.

"If you love those who love you, what benefit is that to you? For even sinners love those who love them. And if you do good to those who do good to you, what benefit is that to you? For even sinners do the same. And if you lend to those from whom you expect to receive, what credit is that to you? Even sinners lend to sinners, to get back the same amount. But love your enemies, and do good, and lend, expecting nothing in return, and your reward will be great, and you will be sons of the Most High, for he is kind to the ungrateful and the evil. Be merciful, even as your Father is merciful."

5. **(Hebrews 4:14–16)** Since then we have a great high priest who has passed through the heavens, Jesus, the Son of God, let us hold fast our confession. For we do not have a high priest who is unable to sympathize with our weaknesses, but one who in every respect has been tempted as we are, yet without sin. Let us then with confidence draw near to the throne of grace, that we may receive mercy and find grace to help in time of need.

6. **(1 John 4:10)** In this is love, not that we have loved God but that he loved us and sent his Son to be the propitiation for our sins.

CHAPTER 5

1. (**John 1:12–13**) But to all who did receive him, who believed in his name, he gave the right to become children of God, who were born, not of blood nor of the will of the flesh nor of the will of man, but of God.

2. (**Romans 8:16–17**) The Spirit himself bears witness with our spirit that we are children of God, and if children, then heirs—heirs of God and fellow heirs with Christ, provided we suffer with him in order that we may also be glorified with him.

CHAPTER 6

1. (**1 Corinthians 12:12**) For just as the body is one and has many members, and all the members of the body, though many, are one body, so it is with Christ.

CHAPTER 7

1. (**John 14:2**) "In my Father's house are many rooms. If it were not so, would I have told you that I go to prepare a place for you?"

2. (**Revelation 22:4**) They will see his face, and his name will be on their foreheads.

CONTINUE THE **CONVERSATION** AS A FAMILY

UNITED

CAPTURED BY GOD'S VISION FOR DIVERSITY

TRILLIA J. NEWBELL

FOR THE GROWN-UPS: *UNITED*

FOR THOSE YOUNGER THAN YOU: *GOD'S VERY GOOD IDEA*